No Blue Food!

Richie Chevat
Pictures by Nate Evans

Aladdin Paperbacks

Aladdin Paperbacks
An imprint of Simon & Schuster Children's Publishing Division
1230 Avenue of the Americas
New York, New York 10020
First Aladdin Paperbacks edition, April 1996
Designed by Chani Yammer and Nancy Widdows
The text of this book was set in 17 point Syntax
Manufactured in the United States of America
10 9 8 7 6 5 4 3 2 1
ISBN: 0-689-80401-6

Hi! It's me—Allegra. Time to get up! I wonder what's for breakfast! I hope it's waffles or cinnamon oatmeal! They're my favorites. *Mmm*!

Oh no—Daddy cooked something new—
BLUE PANCAKES! Mommy says they're good.
Daddy says I should try them. My brother
Rondo says he'll eat a few thousand.

Some new food is good. I've tried red food and pink food and yellow food and green food. But I don't want any blue food—no way!

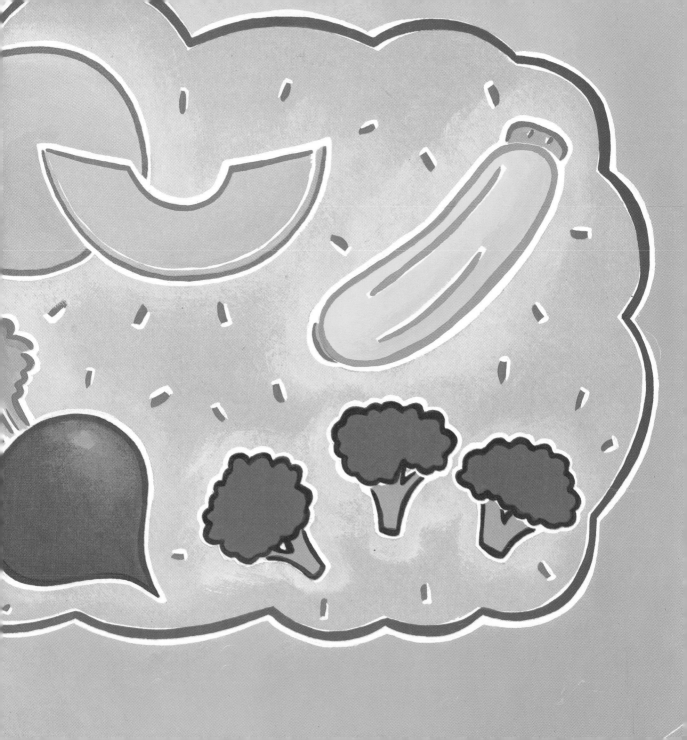

I like lots of *other* things that are blue. My blue overalls are cool! Little Blue Day Care is one of the best places in the whole wide world!

New things are good, too. I try new things at Little Blue every single day.

I've even tried new things when I was scared. When I was two I didn't know how to play any music. Then Reed the music man helped me, and I tried and tried, and now I can!

When I was two and a half I was scared to leave home. But Mommy said it was fun to visit new places. Now I'm three and I love to ride in the car and see great new things like moo-cows and sheep. *Baaaaaa*!

Well, most of the things I see are great. I really am brave, and I'll try lots of new things, but I won't eat yucky new blue food!

These pancakes smell good, though. And I'm pretty hungry. Rondo already ate all of his.

Rondo asks me a question. "If you're not eating yours, may I have them?"

No way! They may be yucky, but they're mine! But Mommy says I have to give them to Rondo if I won't eat them. Now what am I going to do?

I guess I could *try* something new and blue.
Just close my eyes . . . and chew . . . and swallow.
GULP!

Hey! These are yummy! Can I have more?
What's for lunch? I hope it's blue too!

Oh no! Polka dots! No way am I trying polka-dot food!
Would you?